when the EARth Shook

words by Lisa Lucas

pictures by Laurie Stein

Text © 2020 by Lisa Lucas
Illustrations © 2020 by Laurie Stein

Hardcover ISBN 978-0-88448-808-8

First hardcover printing January 2020

Tilbury House Publishers
12 Starr Street
Thomaston, Maine 04861
www.tilburyhouse.com

Library of Congress Control Number: 2019954637

Designed by Frame25 Productions
Printed in China through Four Colour Print Group

15 16 17 18 19 20 XXX 10 9 8 7 6 5 4 3 2 1

The illustrations in this book were created with nontoxic soft pastels on recycled paper, then scanned and Photoshopped

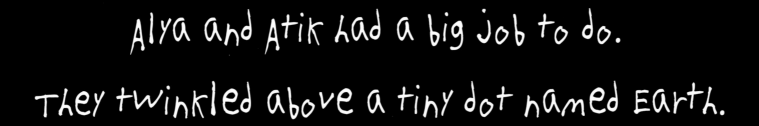

Alya and Atik had a big job to do.
They twinkled above a tiny dot named Earth.

And earth loved their twinkling.

Animals looked up at them.

plants stretched toward them.

And millions of years later, humans traveled across land and sea to gaze and marvel at them.

Centuries passed,
and humans built cars and power plants and
huge factories that spewed out smoke.

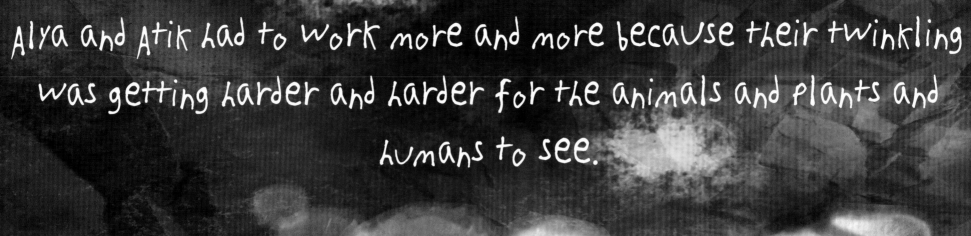

Alya and Atik had to work more and more because their twinkling was getting harder and harder for the animals and plants and humans to see.

Decades passed, and hurricane winds and sooty smoke and blinding light from wildfires spread across Earth.

Alya and Atik had to use every bit of their energy to be seen,
until at last their twinkles could no longer shine
through Earth's smoke and soot and stormy weather.

Alya and Atik
became
frustrated
and
grumpy
and screamed at Earth,

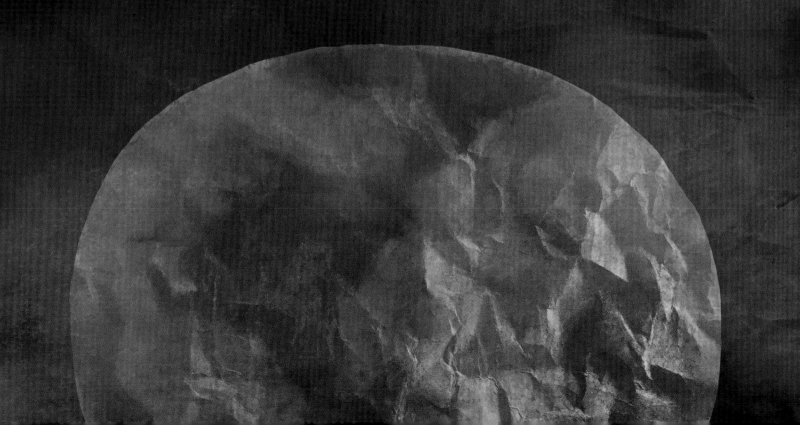

Stunned,
Earth,

who was feeling
hot and sick,
started to cry.

She cried so hard
that she shook.

And she shook.

And the animals,
the plants,
and the humans
were still . . .

except for the king
and a few of his
followers,
who
yelled,

"Okay Earth,
what
is your
problem?!"

Then a little girl named
Axiom
marched up to the king
and told him
to hush.

The king didn't
like that.

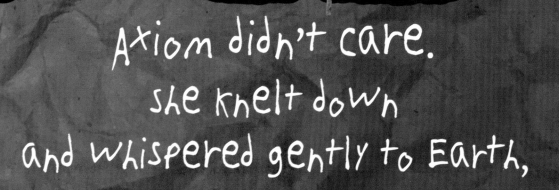

Axiom didn't care.
She knelt down
and whispered gently to Earth,

"can you please stop crying?
we'll all help you."

She grabbed an enormous megaphone.

She told the humans and animals exactly what to do to make Earth feel better.

Everyone listened,
except for the king and just
three of his followers.

And with time, the air cleared
and the water shone blue.

And Earth stopped shaking.

And Alya and Atik
twinkled brightly again.

The animals looked up.
And the plants stretched up.

And all the humans,
except for the king, gazed up and smiled.

Axiom speaks

Axiom picked up her enormous megaphone and took a deep breath. Here is what she said:

"Please, listen. Earth is our home, our only home. And this tiny blue dot among a billion trillion stars, this precious dot we call Earth, is getting hot and sick. If we don't take action, a day will come when Earth can no longer provide enough air, water, or food for us to live. Our only home won't be able to shelter us anymore, and we'll have nowhere to go. Nowhere!

"So I'm begging all of you to become Earth Warriors. It will take effort, time, courage, and hope to win this battle. It will mean changing how we do things.

"As Earth Warriors, we'll fight to keep carbon dioxide out of the air and plastics out of the oceans. We'll stop traveling by air, and we'll walk, ride a bicycle, or take a bus or train instead of driving a car. We won't eat meat, and we'll grow our own food or eat food that's grown locally rather than packaged in plastic or Styrofoam and trucked in from far away. We'll compost, recycle, upcycle, and throw away almost nothing. We won't buy anything we don't need. We'll turn out lights. We'll put on sweaters rather than turning up the heat. We'll plant lots of trees that are native to

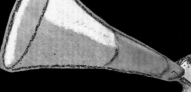

where we live. We'll create habitat for insects, birds, and other wildlife in our yards, and we'll encourage our neighbors and towns to do the same. We'll live in houses that burn no fossil fuels, and we'll ask our towns and cities not to burn them either.

"People before us cleaned up rivers, banned pesticides, and invented recycling. Now it's our turn. As Earth Warriors, we'll use the most powerful weapon there is—our imaginations. We'll use family vacations to care for the environment where we live instead of being tourists somewhere else. We'll take time off from school to join other Earth Warriors in climate activism, because actions are the best form of hope. We'll imagine new ways of doing things that are better for the Earth, and we'll demand that our leaders use their imaginations, too. There will be people who don't like what we say. They'll tell us to stop what we're doing because the Earth is fine. But we know better, so we'll forge ahead no matter what they say, because we will be living our lives for our futures, not theirs."

Earth Warriors reduce their carbon footprints. The ideas in these websites are a good starting point: www.50waystohelp.com | climatekids.nasa.gov

Earth Warriors engage in advocacy and activism to reduce our global carbon footprint, too. Try these sites: www.un.org/en/actnow | 350.org